This Book Belongs To

Gracie's Big Surprise

A Story of Trust And Understanding

By Karen Ravn

Illustrated by Cary Phillips

The leaves were turning red and gold, the weather was turning crisp and cool, and then, at 2:30 on a Thursday afternoon, Granville Groundhog made the big announcement—fall was officially in the air!

After that, each of the animals knew it was time to get busy preparing for winter in his or her own special way.

Brad Badger hurried to finish canning vegetables from his garden. Burl Squirrel started getting serious about his acorn collection.

Priscilla Opossum started knitting a new nightcap...and crocheting a new afghan...and embroidering a new pillowcase.

Benson Bear and the twins Hunky and Dorie started eating (and eating and eating some more!) so they'd be ready for their long winter's nap.

And then there was Gracie Goose. Gracie started helping everybody else with everything they had to do. That was just the thoughtful, lovable kind of goose that Gracie was and one of the reasons everyone liked her! But Gracie also had her own special fall job to do—the biggest, longest, hardest job of all. Gracie had to fly south!

That made Gracie sad. Sure, she loved to fly! Sure, she loved the South! But it was hard to leave the nice homey house and all the nice friendly friends she had right here.

"Of course," Gracie told herself, "I don't have to leave today. Or tomorrow. Or even the day after that. No, I just have to leave sometime pretty soon, but not really, really soon." When she thought about it that way, Gracie felt better. "All I have to do right away," she thought, "is plan my trip, and maybe I can even get Mitzi to help me."

Mitzi was Mitzi Mouse, a very cheery, lively, merry mouse, who was especially good at planning things.

So Gracie set off to see Mitzi, but she decided to visit Oscar Owl at
the library first.

Fritz Frog was there, too, speed-reading a recipe book. (Fritz was very
speedy about everything he did.)

Oscar was standing on a ladder, putting up a special display. "Aha!" he
said when he saw Gracie. "I was just thinking of you!"

"You were?" Gracie asked. It was exciting to think that someone as important and brilliant as Oscar Owl had just been thinking of her!

"I was, indeed," Oscar said. "Indeed, I was. I was thinking that you should be leaving us soon. You should, indeed. Indeed, you should."

"Oh, yes, that," Gracie said. She wished that Oscar had been thinking about how nice she was or how clever she was or, well, almost anything except how soon she had to leave!

"Remember," Oscar said, "they who hesitate are late. That's from my book. You've read my book, haven't you? Would you like to read it again?"

"I'm afraid I don't have time," Gracie said, "if I have to leave so soon."

Then Gracie left the library, but she wasn't in the mood to visit Mitzi anymore, so she went home. "I hope I wasn't rude to Oscar," she thought on the way, "but he was a little rude himself, telling me that I should be leaving like that. He was, indeed. Indeed, he was. But maybe he didn't mean anything by it."

The next day, Gracie set off again to see Mitzi, but she decided to visit Priscilla Opossum first.

Priscilla was busy making a quilt, and Hunky and Dorie were busy watching and munching on honey buns.

"This quilt is for us!" Hunky announced.

"To keep us warm and snug while we're hibernating," Dorie added.

"Hibernating is so great," Priscilla said with a yawn.

"I wish I got to hibernate," Gracie said.

"But you get to fly south," the twins said.

"That's right," Priscilla said. "Gracie SHOULD be leaving any day now."

"I'm in no hurry," Gracie said. She thought Priscilla would understand because Priscilla was never in any hurry to do anything at all!

"But you have to go soon," Priscilla said, "before it gets too cold."

"I suppose," Gracie said.

When Gracie left Priscilla's house, she wasn't in the mood to visit Mitzi anymore, so she went home. "Even Priscilla thinks I should hurry up and leave," she said to herself. "This is starting to hurt my feelings."

The next day Gracie set off again to see Mitzi. But she decided to visit Brad Badger first.

Burl Squirrel and Myra Mole were already there, admiring Brad's latest gardening success, a humongous pumpkin that had just won a humongous trophy.

"That's the biggest trophy I've ever seen!" Burl said.

"And the biggest pumpkin I've ever seen!" Gracie said.

"And Brad's going to make the biggest pumpkin pie anybody's ever seen," Myra said.

"Myra!" Burl said.

"Shhhh!" Brad said.

"Oops!" Myra said.

"What's wrong?" Gracie asked.

"Nothing," Brad said. "I just didn't want to tell you about the pie."

"Why not?" Gracie asked. "I love pie."

"He can't make it until you leave," Myra said.

"Myra!" Burl said.

"Shhh!" Brad said.

"Oops!" Myra said.

"She didn't mean that," Brad said. "She meant I have to wait until the pumpkin is ready, and the pumpkin won't be ready until you leave."

"I see," Gracie said. But she didn't see, not at all. She wasn't in the mood to visit Mitzi anymore, so she went home. "Why won't the pumpkin be ready until I leave?" she asked herself on the way. "It doesn't make sense. I guess Brad doesn't want me to have any pie."

11

The next day Gracie set off again to visit Mitzi. "This time I'm not stopping anywhere else," she told herself, but then she heard music coming from the Snuggle Inn, Felicia Fox's cozy log cabin lodge.

"That sounds like the Forest Tree-o!" Gracie thought. "I'd love to listen to them for a minute." So she went inside, and there they were—Ruby Redbird and Benson Bear and Felicia herself—singing and playing and having a great time. But they quit the instant they saw Gracie.

"We were just leaving," Ruby said.

"Right," Felicia said. "They were just leaving."

"But, Felicia," Benson said, "you promised us bran muffins. They're very good for us, you said."

"Benson!" Ruby said sternly.

"Oh, right, we were just leaving," Benson said.

"Speaking of leaving..." Felicia said, turning to Gracie.

"No, no!" Gracie said. "I don't want to speak of leaving!" And she ran very fast right out of the lodge.

After that, Gracie certainly wasn't in the mood to visit Mitzi anymore, so she went home. "I'll go first thing tomorrow," she told herself. "It's obviously time for me to leave town—everybody seems to think so!"

There was frost on Gracie's lawn the next morning when she set off again to see Mitzi. "This time, I'm really not going anywhere else," she told herself. And she really didn't.

When Gracie arrived, Mitzi was putting away her cool summer clothes and taking out her warm fall ones. "Don't you just love fall?" she said. "I just love fall because I get to wear plaid! And I just love plaid! Don't you just love plaid?"

"Yes, I do," Gracie said, "especially yours." For Mitzi was wearing a lot of plaid right then.

"And also I get to make cheesecake," Mitzi said. "And I just love cheesecake! Don't you just love cheesecake?"

"Yes, I do," Gracie said, "especially yours." For Mitzi made the best cheesecake in the whole world.

"Of course, I make cheesecake all year long," Mitzi said, "but now I can make my special fall cheesecake, and I just love that one. Which reminds me—don't ask why!—when are you heading south?"

"Soon," Gracie said, "very, very soon. Just as soon as I can get ready."

"Can I help?" Mitzi asked. "I'd just love to help you get ready. Wouldn't you just love to have me help? We'll start by making a good plan. I just love to make plans."

Just then there was a loud pounding on the door. Then a very loud voice called, "Is Gracie Goose in there? I absolutely must find her immediately!"

When Mitzi opened the door, there stood Granville Groundhog, all loaded down with books and charts and maps and graphs—and bad news!

"I've been studying and calculating and figuring," he said, "and figuring and calculating and studying, and it's my duty to report that cold weather is coming soon—VERY cold weather coming VERY, VERY soon—and it's my duty to report that Gracie should fly south as soon as possible—by tomorrow, at the latest."

Granville sounded extremely upset. It was enough to give Gracie goose bumps. "But I'm not ready!" she cried.

"Don't worry," Mitzi said. "I'm going to help you."

Then Mitzi hurried home with Gracie, but not before she whispered into Granville's ear, "Spread the word! Tell everyone to hurry!"

16

"First you have to take a nap," Mitzi said when they got to Gracie's house.

"But, Mitzi," Gracie said, "we need to get me ready to go."

"No, you need to rest for tomorrow," Mitzi said. "I need to get you ready. Let's see. I'll get Brad to water your plants. The bears can eat up everything in your kitchen, but that's a good thing for once! I'll get Granville to write up a forecast for your trip. And I'll pack your suitcase…

"You're so good at this," Gracie said. "Maybe just a LITTLE nap, then." After all, it HAD been a long morning, and Gracie DID feel sort of tired, and it WAS going to be a long trip, a VERY long trip. So Gracie took a nap. In fact, she napped and napped and napped all afternoon.

Meanwhile, everyone else in town worked and worked on a special surprise, each in his or her own way. And one by one when they were done, they quietly and carefully sneaked into Gracie's house.

Gracie awoke to the sound of music and happy voices. Surprise! Surprise! She had guests, lots and lots of guests. They were giving her a going-away party!

And it was a great party! The Forest Tree-O performed, and they were great. Oscar read a poem–and it was great. And there was food, food, and more food–and it was all great!

Mitzi had made cheesecake. "It's my special fall one," she said. "Don't you just love it?"

Burl had brought zillions of nuts and Fritz had brought fritters. "No, I've never made them before," he said shyly. "I've never made anything before. But I wanted to make them for you, Gracie."

And Brad had brought the biggest pumpkin pie anybody had ever seen. "I'm sure it would win a prize," he said, "if we were having a contest, I mean."

Gracie was happier than she'd ever been in her life. "So this is why you all wanted me to leave," she said.

"You silly goose," Myra said, "nobody WANTED you to leave!"

"We just knew you'd HAVE to leave sometime," Burl explained.

"So we needed to know WHEN," Felicia added.

"So we could be ready," Mitzi squeaked.

"For the party!" Hunky and Dorie chimed in.

"I just love parties," Mitzi said. "Don't you just love parties?"

"I do," Gracie answered. "Especially this one!"

It was freezing the next morning, but everyone turned out to see Gracie off. "It's my duty to report that the cold front has arrived," Granville announced.

"It has, indeed," Oscar said. "Indeed, it has."

"I guess I'd better get going then," Gracie said.

"Yes, you'd better get going!" Mitzi squeaked. And then she blushed and quickly added, "For your own good, I mean."

Gracie laughed. "I know," she said. "I've learned my lesson. I'll never jump to silly conclusions again."

"Aha!" Oscar said. "Instead of jumping to conclusions, try to clear up your confusions. That's in my book!"

"I'll remember that," Gracie said. "I promise." She turned to the south and spread her wings. "Good-bye, everybody," she said.

"Good-bye, Gracie," they all answered. "We'll miss you." They all watched as she flew up, up, up–high in the sky. "We love you!" Mitzi called after her. And as Gracie looked back one last time, everybody else joined in. "We'll always love you," they cried. "We're your friends!"